I0586321

DRAGON'S HEART

Dragon's Heart

SM Kemmett

The Word Tailor

Dragson's Heart
Original story copyright © 2019 by Sharon M Kemmett
Paperback edition © 2023 by Sharon M Kemmett

The moral right of this author has been asserted.

All rights reserved in all media. No part of this book may be reproduced, stored or transmitted in any form, or by any means, without written permission (except under the statutory exceptions of the Australian Copyright Act 1968).

This is a work of fiction. All characters and events in this publication, other than those clearly in public domain, are fictitious. Any resemblance to real persons, living or dead is purely coincidental.

Cover design, artwork, icons and internal artwork by Karen J Carlisle
ISBN: 978-0-6486500-1-0

 A catalogue record for this book is available from the National Library of Australia

Also available separately as eBook.

This book is written in British English.
Printed in Australia.

Typeset in Times Roman 13pt.

Published by SM Kemmett - Word Tailor.
https://smkemmettwordtailor.wordpress.com/

The Word Tailor

To Karen and David
who have helped so much over many years,
and to Gem
whose friendship I treasure.

CONTENTS

CHAPTER 1

Birch sat cross-legged in the sunlight falling through the door-flap, sewing on the softened deerskins and trying not to hear the sounds of departure as the rest of her People left on the Big Hunt.

A woman scolded her husband for something left behind. His footsteps slapped towards the huts as he hurried to fetch it. Grouse whirred upward. The Shaman, Aesc's father, chanted the last prayers to the gods for many kills.

Birch's father's deep voice gave the order: "Move out!" and many feet rustled through the grasses, falling into the steady pace best for walking long distances.

She was left behind. She could not hunt yet: not before the Shaman returned and the moon had changed. It would bring ill-luck, and perhaps frighten the herds of bison and auroch away.

The voices faded…

Insects took up their chirruping and scratching again. In the near distance, she heard the river bubbling. The wind sighed across the plain thick with new summer grasses and flowers. Birch lay down her work, stretched and wriggled her shoulders. She leaned back on the sun-warmed leather wall of the hut, idly watching the sparks from the small central fire drift upwards through the smoke hole, joining earth to bright blue sky.

It smelled warm and home-like, but Birch, almost alone in the quiet, half-deserted hunting camp, felt like it was a drizzly day. Should she rest, and go and find someone to talk to?

The flattened grass beyond her feet rustled as a stone-coloured lizard poked his head inside the hut. It watched her: She watched it.

"Hungry?" she asked. Would it take food from her? Or was it too timid?

Birch offered a morsel of dried meat to the small dragon-like creature. He stepped closer. Once more. He grabbed the meat, retreated, and looked at her again. His courage made her smile. He scampered off, to take his treasure to safety. So - he was wise, too.

A light, thin music came to her ears: that must be Aesc! She envisioned his lips and his strong, supple fingers drawing the music like magic from the thin bone pipe he had carved. She had no such skill: all she made was squeaks. She shrugged: Aesc could do many things others could not.

As she listened to the melody, she sighed, content, and turned her mind back to her work. This was the handsomest garment she had ever made. She had chosen the softest hide. Last fishing season she had found some fine shells with which to decorate it. It would be worthy of being a wedding gift. If only she got the chance to give it to him…

The fire in the central hearth clicked and spat. The sunlight stretched across the skin-covered floor. Birch's belly rumbled. If she was hungry Aesc must be, too. The sun was high. It was time to take him food.

She put her bone awl and needle away and rose to fill a basket for them to share: left-over meat, nuts, cresses fresh from the river this morning. Birds eggs? There were none left. Well, she would take him some bilberries. He liked berries.

Aesc held a chunk of bone in his palm, and carved it with a sharp stone flake. A glow of satisfaction warmed him as he watched it take on its new shape. The slope of the mammoth's back, its mighty feet and sweeping tusks: It was good work.

He shifted his weight to the other buttock; the pile of furs on which he sat seemed less soft than they had been. He sighed. It was hard to sit still for so long. Would he be more comfortable outside, on the grass, in the fresh air?

The shrine lamp flickered, drawing his eye towards the sacred space on the far side of the hut. The light should not flicker. It should always be strong and bright so the gods would be mindful of them.

He tried his ankle and winced. It was still too stiff for him to stand, so he shuffled across on his bottom, like a seal on the beach.

The stone bowl of the lamp still had plenty of deer fat in it and enough wick.

"Aesc?"

He knew her voice. It made his heart pound like a festival drum. He smiled as he wriggled back towards the centre of the living space and sat in the shaft of sunlight falling through the roof hole. Which should he try: a manly brave face? Or to gain her sympathy, test her feelings for him?

"Birch?"

Birch smiled at the sound of his familiar voice.

"Come in," he said.

Her shadow fell across the ochre designs protecting the walls of Aesc's family's hut. The biggest of the cluster of round dwellings, it must house not only the Shaman's family, but also host the Gods. To Birch, its shape was like that of a woman curled in sleep and great with child. She ducked under its mammoth-bone lintel and entered.

Aesc sat on the floor, one leg stretched out in front of him, his ankle wrapped in stiffened leather, his carving tools beside him.

"Greetings," she said. "I have brought food."

"Thank you." He spread a soft fur for her to sit on, next to him. "You did not join the hunt today…" he said.

"No." Her face warmed. Should she tell him why? Would that be too bold? "I became a woman two se'en-nights ago," she hinted. "I must wait for the Shaman to return for my blessing ritual."

She handed him the basket. "And someone must tend you." She was careful to keep her voice even: he must not feel she blamed him for the wait.

He frowned and his cheeks flushed. "Clumsy oaf that I am, now my aged father hunts in my place." He rummaged in the basket and did not look at her.

She touched his hand, to draw his gaze.

"You hit your mark, though. The beast will taste good."

"It will." Aesc straightened his back and grinned. As he leaned back, he toppled.

She grabbed the basket, and placed it safely, but did not shame him by offering to help him up. Nor did she laugh - until he did.

He shook his head. "You see: clumsy." He chuckled. Their shared laughter faded to smiles.

"No, not clumsy." She understood, she had seen it amongst her friends. And she, herself, became wordless when he was near. It was because her heart was too full. Perhaps his also?

"You are still the greatest spearman amongst our People," she said. He would be a good provider when he married.

His eyes held hers. "Yes." He handed her a large

slice of meat. "I am."

Birch flushed. Had he guessed her thought?

"And you are a woman, now," he added. He did remember her earlier words. "Congratulations, Birch." He leaned down and kissed her on the cheek.

"Thank you, Aesc," she said. She offered him the basket. He took some meat and nuts.

They ate in silence. Birch could think of nothing to say. Had she said too much already – hinting that she was now old enough to marry? Why did Aesc not say anything? Usually, they always knew what to say to each other. Perhaps she had misread the signs. Perhaps he didn't think of her as she'd hoped -

He took the basket from her hands and placed it aside. He leaned towards her, slowly. She sensed she could move away, if she wished. She did not. He kissed her, and she made a trial of returning his kiss. She relaxed into his arms. What a fool she'd been; she must learn to trust her instincts.

He brushed her hair back from her face and searched her eyes.

"Birch, I have loved you and waited for two years for you to be grown. Will you be my woman?"

"Yes," she whispered. Her heart wanted to fly from her body, to shout, to sing. How could she sound so calm?

Aesc struggled to stand up. He winced and plopped back to the floor.

"There is a satchel in the corner there," he said, "Would you fetch it for me?"

She handed it to him. He unfolded the soft fur, and

lifted out a string of polished amber beads. It was as though dawn dripped from his fingers. "Wife, accept this gift as token of my love."

He fastened the necklace on for her, and then kissed her neck. The touch of his lips filled her blood with feelings she had no words for yet. She embraced him, returned his kisses.

When they parted, she looked at his gift. It was beautiful. How many beaches had he walked to collect these sea-borne stones? What had he traded for them? She lifted them to her nose and inhaled the breath of sun warmed pine trees and honey as her skin warmed the beads.

"I accept your gift, and give my love."

CHAPTER 2

The sun edged towards the skyline. The fire burned lower in the hearth, but they were warm in each other's arms.

Birch snuggled up with Aesc, barely able to keep her eyes open. She heard his heart beat, slow and strong, felt his chest under her fingers as it rose and fell with his breathing. His arm embraced her. Birch was where she belonged, where she was fated to be. She closed her eyes and drifted into sleep.

The ground sank under her feet. Cold water oozed up from the moss. Midges swarmed in clouds, biting. A dragonfly, its body as sharp as a needle, flew at her eyes, its sparkling wings blinding her. Sinking, she reached out for Aesc.

Heart pounding, breathless, she heard him.

"Birch, wake up." He held her, rocked her. "Do you

want to tell me about it? My father is teaching me to interpret."

She shook her head. "It was just a dream. It has gone now."

Aesc stroked her hair until she slept again.

Distant voices of returning hunters roused Birch from her sleep. She still lay in Aesc's embrace, her cheek on his soft arm. She looked into his face, not wanting to move. His eyelids fluttered open.

"Good morning, love," he whispered.

"Good morning, husband," she smiled. "Whose folk shall we tell first?" She yawned and stretched.

Aesc did not answer; he stared past her. His arm fell from her body as he sat up.

"The fire!" He swallowed.

Birch looked at the dull glow in the central hearth. True, it burned a little low, but what of that? There was plenty of fuel stacked nearby.

Aesc gently turned her face away from the big hearth towards the little flame in the shrine.

Her stomach turned over. "Oh, no!"

"Get dressed. I will kindle it again." He hobbled to the shrine.

She tugged her tunic on and joined Aesc. The oil in the lamp bowl was almost gone. The short wick sagged against the bowl's side, flickering, gasping for life. Aesc grabbed a new wick and held it against the old. He breathed on them both, praying the flame would take. Birch dripped more oil in from the other side.

She blinked back threatening tears. It was bad enough to let a cooking fire go out, but the shrine-hearth, that was holy... It was an insult to the Sky Gods that sent it. It meant ill-luck, perhaps even a famine, for the house, or even for the whole village.

The hides over the door were folded back. Aesc's father ducked under the flaps and entered. Stepping to the middle of the hut, his gaze sought Aesc. He looked at the rumpled bed place, at them, and at the flame-empty shrine. His black eyebrows knotted.

"The fire is out." The Shaman's voice was quiet, but Birch shivered.

"Yes, father," said Aesc. "I am sorry."

The Shaman turned to her and scowled. "You may go, Birch."

She bowed, not meeting his glare, and slunk past the hearth towards the door. Her mother, the Seeress, and her father, the Chieftain, entered. Birch stepped back for them.

Mother's eyes met those of the Shaman and followed his gaze.

"Aesc, take what you need and await our decision at the outskirts," commanded her mother. "You, too, Birch."

Tears pricked behind Birch's eyes. As she turned to go, her mother rested a hand on her arm and glanced at Birch's amber necklace.

"You and Aesc?" Birch held her breath and nodded.

"Good." Her mother smiled and reached out to touch

the beads. Birch felt a jolt, her skin tingled. Her mother had gone, the Seeress looked out of her eyes

"Be careful. When you lose this gift, you may lose your husband with it," said the Seeress.

"I will never lose it!" declared Birch.

Her mother's eyes smiled at her. Birch felt no more tingling.

Not knowing what else to do, she picked up the basket of fruit. Her father gripped her wrist, took the basket from her.

"No. You let the fire starve; it is just that the two of you starve a little, too. Take a waterskin, your furs and a knife. We will call you both when we have talked."

Aesc walked with her from the hunting camp in silence.

Birch sat next to Aesc on a hillock and looked down on the dwellings clustered along the river beach. The round shapes covered in red-brown mammoth hides looked like so many bubbles rising to the surface of the cooking pot, but their entrances, edged by the beasts' own tusks, looked like hungry mouths.

Aesc stood silent, and stared at the ground. Birch shivered. What would the elders decide?

"Will we be punished?" Birch asked Aesc. His father was the Shaman; Aesc would know these things.

"Yes." He sat beside her and placed his arm around her shoulders.

12

Her stomach fluttered. She hoped she would not be sick in front of Aesc. "What will they do?"

"I do not know. Perhaps they will beat us, or wound us. Perhaps they will banish us. Who knows? Do not be afraid. I will take the punishment. It was my fault."

"No. You are my man, now. I slept under your cloak; I will take my own punishment, with you."

Aesc took her cold hand in his. It helped calm her. A little.

"It's time," Aesc helped her to her feet. The Shaman, the Chief and the other elders drew near. The Shaman spoke to them:

"This do we say: you will leave this place and seek the Sky Gods. You will make them a sacrifice and beg their forgiveness for the insult you gave them. When you return, bring with you the new holy fire in token of that forgiveness."

Aesc's mother and Birch's aunt brought them food and all the things needful for their journey. Birch looked for her mother, but she was not there, and Birch's throat ached.

"Your mother is the Seeress." Her aunt placed her gentle hand on Birch's shoulder and spoke softly. "She speaks with the spirits and the fates about the outcome of your journey."

Birch nodded. The Seeing must come first. Her aunt kissed her.

"Be safe," she said, and was gone. Birch watched her leave until a sound made her turn.

Ulv, Aesc's best friend stood there.

"I brought you this," he said, "To keep you safe

and protected in your going…" He moved to place the gift around her neck: a wolf-shaped ivory amulet on a leather thong.

"Thank you, Ulv. How thoughtful! But I cannot accept your gift. I am sorry."

"Why not, Birch?"

"Well, I am married."

"Married?" He dropped his hand.

"Yes. Aesc and I – last night."

His smile wobbled. He flushed. "Oh. He had not told me." The smile settled, brightened. "How wonderful, Birch. You will make Aesc happy. I am glad for you both."

"Thank you," She smiled as she closed his hand over the wolf ornament.

"Will you not keep it? Aesc will not mind – we've been friends since boyhood. Think of it as a wedding gift. For you both."

Birch hesitated, then nodded, letting him replace the amulet. She had been friends with Ulv almost as long as with Aesc.

"I will say farewell to Aesc," he said as he moved away. "Go safely, Birch."

Aesc was speaking with his brother; they shook hands and parted. Ulv, with a grin, shook Aesc's hand, and Aesc farewelled him with a hug. He picked up his hunting spears with the Shaman's blessing marks still damp on them, and walked towards Birch.

Her father reached her first.

"It saddens me to send you away, daughter," he said. "The fire ritual can be remade by the Shaman from another fire, but the blasphemy must still be repaired."

"I understand, father."

"That is my brave girl."

Birch stared at the ground, and swallowed. "I do not feel brave; I am afraid to go into lands I do not know."

"Yet you go, anyway. That is what makes you brave."

"Aesc goes with me," Aesc had joined them, and stood by her side. She took his hand. She hesitated. "Father, we are -"

"I know. It is a good match. We will make your wedding feast when you return." He reached out and clasped Aesc's hand in welcome.

"Have you wisdom for us, sir? How shall we know the gods if we find them?"

"Gods are like the wind. Unless they will it, you cannot see them, but you can see what they do."

Aesc nodded.

"Birch…" Her father's voice was husky, he stroked Birch's hair, but found no words. He laid a hand briefly on Aesc's shoulder.

"Now, go," her father said, his voice stern; he was the clan's Chieftain once again.

CHAPTER 3

They turned away from the hunting camp.

"Which way do we go?" said Birch. "Where do the sky gods live?"

Aesc shrugged. "Towards the rising sun?" he suggested, looking Eastward across the plain. Grandfather had told him of ice-rivers in the lands towards the dawn. Could they to get beyond them, to where the sun rose?

"Or upward into mountains?" she suggested.

Aesc considered. "Our winter camp lies south and east; we know those lands -"

"Then we go north-west, across the plain, into the uplands."

Aesc nodded and hoisted his pack and his gathering bag onto his shoulders. Birch did likewise. They started off across the grassy lowland, towards the forested foothills that were said to lie many days' journey away.

The wind soughed forever over the grass, tossing it like waves of the sea. The distant northern sea itself was a silver line between earth and sky. Wildflowers and low plants were scattered through the marshland. Some were good to eat, so they stopped and gathered them when they could.

Birch reached for her bag. Stopped. The bag moved.

"Aesc, there's something alive in my bag," she said, "Suppose it is a serpent?"

Aesc searched the ground, found a sturdy stick. "Suppose it is a mouse?" he countered. He handed her the stick anyway.

There was only one way to find out: Birch opened the mouth of the bag, keeping well back. Reptilian eyes peered out at her. Delicate claws shone in the sunlight.

"Oh! My little friend!" she knelt and picked up the small lizard.

"What?" Aesc said.

"He visited me before we left camp. So, little Dreki, do you want to come with us? Want us to hunt for you?"

Dreki ran up her arm and perched on her shoulder, holding tight to her hair.

One bright morning they chose a river flowing north west across the plains and followed it up stream. The land began to slope upwards, becoming hilly. One day, they passed the first tall tree, bravely standing against the constant wind of the plains. White cliffs stood between them and the forested uplands. They looked for a low place at which they could scale them.

Birch woke. A cold heaviness clutched her heart like a snow drift. She had been dreaming, but what about?

Something bad. Something terrible was coming.

She sat up. Aesc still slept, the hint of a smile on his lips. She was glad his dreams were pleasant. It was too early to wake him. Needing to relieve herself, she scrambled from her furs and sought a nearby tree. Feeling better, at least in body, she returned to their sleeping place, pausing to take a deep breath before she laid down.

The sky was black, and bright with stars. As she gazed upward, one star fell earthward, followed by another. More white sparks filled the northern sky. They blazed, bright and brilliant, trailing long fiery tails.

"Aesc, the stars are falling!" She shook his shoulder. "Look, Aesc!"

"What?" he rubbed his eyes, and looked where she pointed. "Oh. My Grandfather said those are dragons, migrating."

One, larger than the rest, fell flaming. Somewhere, far away, it must have crashed to the ground, for they heard a boom, as loud as a thunder bolt.

The tremor rippled towards them, until the earth shook under their feet. Trees swayed, their leaves pattering to the ground with a sound like rain. The howl of a frightened wolf came from deep in the woods. Birds rose, startled from sleep, calling alarms.

Dread still clung to Birch. She rubbed her tingling fingers together. In her mind, she heard a silent keening, filled with grief. Tears ran down her face and she did not know why. Aesc held her close.

"What is it, beloved? What happened to you? Did you see something?"

She looked up into his face. What did he mean by that? Had he guessed something?

She bit her lip. She did not want to think of it. That was for later.

Drying her eyes, she pointed north. "We need to go that way: far. We must follow the dragons."

"How do you know?"

"I just know. They will help us find the Sky Gods. Perhaps they are sky gods. Come, Aesc. I can sleep no more, anyway. We might as well walk."

"In the dark?"

"Yes. Come." She grabbed some of their gear and started walking. Aesc kicked out the remains of the fire, collected the rest, and followed.

The forest thickened. When it was time to build a shelter each evening, they set snares for small animals and birds to add to their stores.

While Birch checked their snares, Aesc looked for larger game. He found deer prints and followed them. Soon after, the prints were joined by others: wolf!

The deer had not been dead long. The blood smelt fresh. Wolf paw prints surrounded the carcass, and led away, into the deep woods. There was plenty of meat left. A raven called from a nearby tree.

Aesc cut into the deer's hide and slid the flint blade flat under the skin. The raven flew to the ground, hopped a little closer. Aesc cut up towards the animal's heart, wondering just how bold the black bird would be.

"I see you there, friend. Yes, I will give you a share."

"Kaa," said the he-raven.

"The wolf left enough meat for three."

Another raven hopped up beside the first. "Kaa kaa."

"Ah, I am sorry." He laughed, "Enough for four."

He threw them some gobbets of meat, bundled up the rest, and returned to Birch at their shelter and fire-side. The ravens followed him; it seemed they had decided to join them in the journey. That night Aesc built the fire up extra high but the wolf did not harass them.

The ravens went with them the next day. The he-raven often darted in front, while the she-raven remained close to Aesc. "You like to fly ahead, as fast as thought." Aesc said to the male bird, "I shall call you 'Hugin', which is 'Thought' in my speech."

He looked at the female, who liked to stay behind with him, and often perched on his shoulder. "And you will be 'Munin', 'Memory' because you stay with me. Is that well with you?"

Munin, already perched on his shoulder, rubbed

his face with her beak; Hugin flew up onto his other shoulder.

"I think they approve," said Birch.

Birch curled up, hugging herself. Her teeth chattered. She barely remembered the sun. The black sky covered it. The ice was coming, the sky was torn. A wolf with two heads swallowed the sun. Its other maw devoured the moon. She moaned. So cold...

The she-raven watched as a wisp of light rose up from Birch's amulet and drifted towards the floor of the clearing. It stretched upward, became solid and changed into a man. He leaned towards Birch's ear and whispered:

"My dearest Birch, this journey is too hard for you. You are so tired. You must tell Aesc that you wish to go home."

Birch stirred; the man stepped back, watching her. She turned over, but did not wake. Munin cawed in alarm and the man's eyes searched the branches for her. She stayed still and silent. The man turned to mist again, and taking the shape of a wolf, shook itself and loped off, disappearing amongst the trees.

Their travels took them closer to the sea again. Foraging from both woodland and sea, they had food in abundance. Birch lifted her face to the sunlight streaming through the leaves and felt the sea-breeze ruffle her hair. While they stayed near the coast they feasted on fish, fowl and sometimes deer; on birds and seaweed, shellfish, eggs and herbs. Birch crunched on a burdock root, and watched Aesc. He had not moved for some time. She resisted the urge to check that he was still breathing; of course he was.

"What are you looking at, Aesc?" she whispered, so as not to disturb him.

"A honey bee," he eased to a sitting position. "And where there is one bee, there are many…"

She followed Aesc as he tracked the insect; it was soon joined by others. They searched and as they hoped, found a bees' nest in a hollow of an old ash tree.

"Look – there," said Aesc. He slung a spare bag over his shoulder, strode toward the tree, and climbed.

Birch looked past where he had pointed, to the sky beyond: it was clouding over.

"Aesc, must you go now? It is going to rain. Look, even the bees know and huddle in their nest."

"That will make the honey easier to get."

Birch frowned. Reckless, that is what Aesc was! Could he not see that rain was coming?

Aesc broke off some outside combs, put them in the bag, and dropped it down to Birch.

The sky darkened. Clouds scudded inland. Rain spattered them. Aesc, on his way down, slipped on the slick bark. He dropped an arm's length, and small branches broke around him, scratching his flesh and snagging his clothes. One of Aesc's feet hit a branch. Another branch clutched at his tunic, dragging it up tight around his neck. He hung on, feeling for better footing, found it, and climbed down.

As he dropped to the ground, lightning struck the tree. Above, a big branch exploded. Spear-like shards of bark pierced Aesc as an invisible hand knocked him to the earth. Birch was knocked clear and landed flat on her back, winded.

Birch kneaded her belly, and gasped for breath. She tried to sit up. Pain stabbed her. Where was Aesc? She spotted him nearer to the tree. She crawled towards him, struggled to her feet, and helped him up. He had a deep cut above his eye, which was already beginning to swell shut. Blood and rain ran down his face.

"C- can you walk?" she gasped.

He nodded. Putting her arm around him, she helped him move. They two stumbled through the forest. They had to find shelter.

Lightning flashed: Birch flinched, her heart pounded. Paleness showed between the trees. They limped towards it. A rocky crag rose ahead of them. A patch of darkness broke the rock face. A cave? Heartbeat quickening, she hoped so.

"Wait here," she said. She leaned Aesc against a tree, grabbed one of his spears, and edged towards the outcrop.

Birch halted, bent and picked up a stone with her other hand. She threw the stone into the darkness and heard it thud twice. She guessed it had hit the back of the cave and its floor. Nothing rushed out. No bear, no cave lion. Her breath hissed in relief. She helped Aesc towards the sparse shelter.

The cave was shallow, little more than a rocky overhang, but someone had stayed here before; stones formed a hearth, and there was dry wood stacked nearby. The ravens flew in with them and found places to perch. They shook rain from their feathers. Once out of the wind, her cold, wet skin felt warmer.

Birch wiped the blood from Aesc's eye, crushed plants in a bowl of water, applied the poultice to his eye, and bound it to his brow. She examined his other wounds. He hissed from pain when she pulled out the shards of bark from his body but she bathed the wounds with birch sap.

"That feels better," he sighed.

"Good." She brushed his lips with a careful kiss.

Lightning still cracked overhead. Birch frowned. What had they done to offend the Sky Gods this time? Were the thunder and lightning mocking her? Here is your fire: Take it if you can!

Was the tree still burning? The rain was so hard it would quench the fire, anyway. Perhaps that was a good thing? Wild forest fires were a bad death.

Birch dropped her head onto her hands. If they failed in their quest Aesc would lose face and the elders would consider him unworthy of a Seeress' daughter. Would the Elders separate them?

Her hand went to her throat; the touch of her necklace reassured her, reminded her of Aesc's love. Her fingers clutched at her neck. Her stomach twisted. The necklace was not there!

She remembered her mother's words: 'When you lose that necklace, you may lose your husband.' She would not let it happen. She would heal Aesc, and they would succeed in their search. Even if they had to leave the clan and live in Aesc's Grandfather's country, banished from the People, they would not be parted.

She brushed her husband's forehead as he slept. The tension in her brows relaxed: There was no fever. Aesc slept, looking peaceful. She kissed his cheek and crept from the cave. The rain slapped her. With each lightning flash she searched the forest floor for her necklace. Munin hopped from branch to branch as if to help her.

Thunder crashed closer. A golden glow glinted in the leaf matter. There! Birch grabbed the string of amber, tucked the beads safely inside her neckline again and clutched them tight as she hurried back to Aesc.

She clasped his hand and settled down to sleep beside him. The storm passed, the thunder rumbled away into the distance.

CHAPTER 4

The pine forest was becoming thicker as they moved north and upwards.

"I won't be able to hunt until my eye heals, Birch."

"No," she agreed.

That was well while they were amongst the woods, - there was plenty to forage, - but they would soon have to rely on scavenged or hunted meat, or river fish.

"You are quick and light on your feet, and you learn fast. I will teach you to hunt with the spear."

"Me?" she asked.

"Why not?"

He chose his light spear, and made her practice aiming at logs. Then he walked with her through the trees, saying "Hit that," and "Try for that hare."

He made her practice every day. Slowly she became

competent, and then skilled.

One time, Munin came flying back to them. He landed silently on Aesc's shoulder, and tugged at his hair.

"Something that way?" Aesc murmured. "Something to eat?"

"Kaa."

They crept forward, and peered through the undergrowth. Munin spoke truth: a small herd of deer browsed in a clearing. Aesc beckoned to Birch. Placing her feet silently, she came up next to him.

Choosing the smallest animal, since there were only two of them to feed, (and the birds and Dreki) she drew her spear arm back. This young beast, lacking wisdom, had strayed from its fellows: Birch's spear found its mark.

The herd scattered, their quarry fled with them. Birch and Aesc followed.

By the time they had tracked it to where it had fallen, the sun was well past noon.

Aesc showed her where to cut, to speed the deer's journey into the next life. When it was done, he laid a gentle hand on the animal's flank.

"It is a dread thing, one's first kill," said Aesc to Birch. "It is right that we thank the beast that gives its life that we may live."

"Thank you," Birch whispered. Her voice was hoarse, and her hands shook.

They cut off as much meat as they could carry, and gave the rest back to the Earth Mother who gave it. They would eat well for many days.

The moon waned, and waxed. The land grew steeper, pine trees, spruce and juniper covered the hills, filling the air with cool fresh scents that Birch breathed in deeply. The summer nights were short, but each felt cooler than the last as they ascended the slopes. To the west were mountains. Sometimes, when the clouds cleared, Birch could see snow on the highest peaks.

That night Birch brewed a hot drink of pine needles for them. Her mother always said it strengthened the body, and kept off the winter fevers that brought constant sneezing. They ate tasty fungi, and snared two grouse. Their water skins had been full at their last stop, and that was good; the river had cut itself into a deep ravine. Birch could hear the water splash and gurgle below. The trees sighed and scraped above them.

The humans slept. Her mate slept. Munin did not sleep. Mist lay close to the ground. Eyes shone in it: wolf eyes. Enemy.

Munin watched as the wolf padded into the trees. She followed.

The wolf ran beside the long water that splashed between the high rocks. Stopped, sniffed.

A tree lay down, one end on this side of the water's path, one end on the other. He sniffed the tree. He put his paws on the tree: front paws, back paws. He ran along it, looked and sniffed at the far end and came back.

He dug around and under the end of the tree. The

ground fell into the water below. The tree quivered.

Aesc looked at the claw marks on the ground, at the branches that lay scattered about, at the log bridge that lay askew below, half in and half out of the water, wedged in the river rocks. Was it an animal that destroyed the log bridge? It made no sense. Or a man? And why would either do such a thing?

He looked at Birch. "We will have to find another way."

"Perhaps the river will be narrower further upstream…" she suggested.

"I hope so," he shook his head. "Gods willing, we may find a fording place soon. Then we can turn north again. We may even meet the makers of this bridge: perhaps they know about the dragons."

"Yes, gods willing." Birch hoped the sky gods were also patient. This could take them far out of their way. She picked up her pack and they started trudging west again.

They had run out of land, all but a few rocky islands. On the largest, a mountain rose out of the sea in front of them. From its peak smoke breathed out. Steam hissed from fissures in the black earth. The island was edged in greenery, and seabirds crowded the rocky beaches. This must be the abode of dragons. But how could they get there?

Birch looked around her.

"What is that?" she pointed at the round object that bobbed in a nearby tidal pool. It was shaped like a cockle shell, and floated like one of their dugout boats. It was made of branches and skins.

Aesc looked around. "Look," he murmured. Someone watched them from the cover of the trees.

"Greetings," called Aesc. "Do you know our words?"

The bright eyes of the youth remained wary. He made no move towards them.

"Is this your boat?" asked Birch.

The boy moved then, stepping out of his cover towards them. He was holding a well-made spear. He strode towards the boat and planted the butt of his spear on it. Clearly, it was his boat.

His body was covered in drawings, whether of plants or animals, Birch could not tell. They must be strong magic.

Aesc lay his spear on the ground, displayed empty hands. Birch did the same.

Aesc knelt and made marks in the dark sand with his finger. The boy watched, seeming intrigued. So did Birch.

"We…" he drew two stick figures in the sand, "… want to go to the smoking mountain island." He drew the island, with the two of them on it. "We will give you a gift," he drew himself, with open hands, offering something. "If we can borrow your boat." He drew a half circle under them.

The boy was listening; he had turned his spear point downwards.

"In three days," Aesc held up three fingers, and drew three suns on the beach. "We will bring your boat back," He rubbed out the figures by the island, and drew them again, next to a drawing of the painted boy. "And we will give you another gift." He drew that.

"Do you agree?"

The Painted boy looked at them, as if deciding. Then he held out his hand for the first gift.

"Birch, what have we got to trade?"

They gave him meat, two spear heads and a bone needle. He seemed satisfied, and handed Aesc the paddle of the coracle. He stood watching them, leaning on his spear, as they tried to get into the little boat and Aesc attempted to paddle.

He got nowhere, only spinning around and around. The boy chuckled, but he showed Aesc how it should be done. Laughing, but red-faced, Aesc got the trick of it.

"Farewell," Birch raised her hand. "We will see you again in three days."

They splashed into ankle deep water and drew the little coracle onto the far shore, pulling it up beyond the high tide mark. There were more plants on the island than had been on the mainland. Birch trees thrust their roots into rich soil. Sea birds squawked in the air.

Birch pointed out to sea.

"Look, Aesc - seals." Birch's stomach choice that moment to rumble. She giggled.

"There will be good hunting for a while." Aesc comforted her. She nodded agreement. They hunted together now, even though his eye was healed. She grinned at him and he smiled back: she loved to hunt by his side, working together to feed each other. They had become a team.

They must have been getting closer to the dragons' home, for the heat seeped from the ground and through their foot coverings. Sometimes, through cracks in the ashy soil, wisps of steam rose up, looking like the breath of dragons in caves below.

A strange smell wafted through the low trees; sharp, foul. Grandfather would say it was Trolls' bath water. Aesc wondered what it really was.

CHAPTER 5

When the sun set at last and the western sky darkened, the northern skyline still glowed, as though rimmed by fire.

From a place of hiding, they lay on their stomachs and watched the dragons wheeling, turning, flying, black against the green Northern lights, glinting with reflected colours against the dark. Flashes of russet and white lit the sky.

Below them a long hollow was gouged in the ground. Was it the place where the dragon had fallen? Within it the earth still burned. Something glowed red hot in its centre.

The side of the mountain was riddled with caves. Between them and the nearest cave mouth a large, dark shape paced. Its scales were black and shiny and sharp as the stones Aesc's father used to make the Ritual knife. Long wings were folded along its back.

"How does one speak to dragons?" wondered Birch, speaking low.

"Respectfully…"

"Hmm…"

Was Aesc afraid? She could not tell by his face. This was the biggest animal either of them had ever seen. Her heart was beating fast, but her stomach did not roil as it did when she was afraid of ordinary things. Perhaps this was awe that she felt, this joy and fear mingled?

Little Dreki emerged from his hiding place in her hood, just far enough to rub his face against her chin. He stared at the dragon. If she was awed by this immense beast, how would it seem to Dreki? He was the same length as just one of the black dragon's white teeth. And yet, Dreki had come out to look. He was right: she could do this even if she was afraid.

The black dragon lifted its muzzle, turned its face towards them. It had scented them. Birch took Aesc's hand and they left their hiding and stood where the guarding dragon could see them.

"Hail, great one, child of the fires of the earth," Aesc said.

"Hail, ruler of the sky," said Birch.

"Who is there?" The dragon turned its long head and looked at them. Its eyes glowed like embers.

"I am called Aesc."

"I am Birch."

They stood still as the enormous creature inspected them.

"Hail, Aesc. Hail, Birch. What do you here?"

"We wish to find our gods of the sky. Can you guide us to them?"

"No," he said. "But I do not know all things. I will speak to Great Mother for you."

He departed towards one of the caverns.

They waited until the dragon re-emerged. "She will speak with you. Follow."

The dragon caves' mouths were filled with gold, shining light. Natural light green gemstones sparkled in the rock walls of the caves. Enthralled, Birch reached out to touch the shiny things.

"Don't, Birch," Aesc warned. He was right, she knew. They must not take, or even touch, them. Not that she would: but they were beautiful.

Birch felt her hands tingle. She shut her eyes, her mind. A dream was coming and she could not stop it. She let Aesc get a few paces ahead of her, and leaned on the wall until the vision had passed. She caught up with him, but told him nothing. The black dragon led them deeper into the mountain.

Great Mother lay curled in the innermost cavern. She lifted her head to examine them. Yards of tail cradled her eggs.

Their guide announced them and their errand and withdrew.

"We seek the gods of the sky. Are you they?" asked Birch. Her fingers were tingling so much she could hardly hold them still.

"Perhaps. What do you want with the sky gods?"

"We come to pay you honour, and ask forgiveness," said Birch.

"Forgiveness? What evil have you done?"

Aesc then told her how they had neglected the holy fire and risked the People, how they had travelled far to ask the gods to restore the flame to them.

"What gift do you ask for atonement?" Aesc asked the dragon.

Great Mother regarded them with unblinking eyes. "I must think about it, come back tomorrow."

They retired to the coast, where there were trees for shelter and good hunting in the form of fish and seals. The two ravens, who had not gone with them – they had kept out of the way of the dragons - flew up to greet them now.

On the morrow, they returned to the fiery mountain.

The dragon matriarch had thought about her answer. As her stomach rumbled, she said: "I have hunger."

"We will hunt meat for you," said Birch.

"You will hunt for me, man, today and tomorrow. The woman shall stay with me."

Aesc made his way around the crater in front of the caves. How could he hunt anything larger than a mouse, alone, without Birch to help him? He walked towards the sea.

His eyes were on the uneven ground as he thought. A sound, a growl, made him look up. His eyes met those of an enormous wolf. He felt his heart halt, squeezed in his chest.

The wolf leapt.

Its weight knocked Aesc from his feet. He fell backwards. A faint wolf musk and meaty breath enveloped him. He felt rough fur. Claws scraped his shoulders, teeth closed around his neck.

And stopped.

The wolf rolled off him, and stood panting.

Aesc raised his spear.

The wolf shimmered, dissolved. A man stood in his place.

"Do you plan to kill me and feed me to the dragons, my friend?" he said.

"Ulv!" The hot sweat on Aesc's skin turned cold. He was glad he was already lying down: he had no knees. "How did you come here? Have you been following us?"

"Yes."

Aesc rolled over, knocked Ulv from his feet and clouted him several times. He also called him all the insulting names he could think of.

Ulv laughed. "So, how is the hunting, friend?" he grinned.

"Look at me, daughter," said Great Mother.

Birch was not sure if she dared. The dragon's golden-green eyes were each as big as her head, and glittered like the crystals in the cave walls. Birch had heard it said that dragons could see yesterday, today, and tomorrow, because of those eyes.

"You have dreams, too, I think," said the dragon. "Like your mother."

Birch remembered she had flinched and turned away from the painful brightness in the tunnels.

"Do not run from the visions," said the dragon. "Embrace them! Where is your courage, Birch? You whose son will be the most beloved of the gods, you who will weave the fates of men and women, who will teach magic to a god. What did you see?"

"A man, tall, with hair the colour of the sun and eyes the shade of the summer sky. His skin is like the clouds flushed with sunset. He is like a god… a wolf comes…"

"I see many, many summers between you and this dream," said the dragon. "And none."

Birch nodded. Strange words. Visions were sometimes hard to understand. "When will I know the meaning of this dream?"

"I cannot say," the dragon admitted. She paused to adjust the placing of one of her eggs. Satisfied, she looked at Birch again.

"What is that that shines at your neck?" she asked Birch.

What? Birch blinked. Her neck? Her hand went up to touch the amber necklace, the wedding gift from Aesc.

"It looks like sunlight turned to stone…" purred the dragon.

Birch's stomach twisted; she felt cold all over. No. Do not ask that.

"You seek the flame. I will give it, if you give me the light that shines around your neck."

Birch could say nothing. Give up Aesc's gift? It would feel like losing him. She could not. But they had come all this way for the holy fire. Her People needed it. They came first.

Had her mother felt this way when she had let her only daughter leave without saying goodbye? Had she known Birch would find the quest so hard?

Birch laid the amber before the Dragon. It felt like giving up her heart.

Aesc's head nodded. His supper bowl tilted in his hands. Birch took it from him and put it next to hers, to wash them later. She spread out their sleeping furs and tucked Aesc into them, snuggling in beside him. She was asleep almost as soon as he was.

Ulv hunted with Aesc again the next day. The dragon had relished the first seal Aesc had brought her, and hoped for another. The sun was high in the sky when they finally got one. By the time it was gutted and they had washed in the sea, their stomachs felt hollow. Aesc handed Ulv one of the roasted birds Birch had sent for them.

"She is a good cook, your wife," said Ulv, tearing at a wing with his teeth.

"Yes,"

"And beautiful."

"I know. Are you going to eat that?"

"Yes, what else would I do with it? Use it as a hat? Wear it around my neck?"

"Fool." Aesc laughed.

'Birch does not think me a fool," he bristled.

"I've known you longer." Aesc grinned, and shoved him.

"Not that much longer. We have all been - close."

Aesc looked at him. His skin prickled. Ulv seemed in a strange mood.

"Birch wears my amulet around her neck. Has she lost your necklace?"

"No. Of course not. She wears it all the time."

"Of course." Ulv smiled a knowing smile. Aesc frowned.

"What are you hinting at?"

"Nothing, friend. Surely you are right. I just thought – last night – she did not wear it."

"How would you know? I do not believe you."

Ulv's mouth drooped at the corners. He did not look at Aesc. "I understand if you want to send us away. Find a wife, and a friend, worthier of you."

Aesc got to his feet. Did Ulv think these words were a good joke?

If so, Ulv's humour irked him. He would listen to no more of it.

"We must get this meat to the dragon," he said.

He lifted one end of the big sea animal, but Ulv did not lift the other. Aesc looked around. Ulv was not there.

Aesc presented the meat to the Mother dragon. She sniffed it and nodded.

"It is good."

"Great Mother, for two days I have hunted for you. Will you now grant us the holy flame, as we agreed?"

"I will. Follow."

She rose and paced before them from the cavern. They followed her to the entrance of the caves.

"See there." The dragon pointed to the bottom of the crater. "There lies my mate, who fell from the skies too soon. Take his heart. Cherish it as I did. Take it to your People."

Together Birch and Aesc descended into the centre of the crater and approached the dragon's heart. Heat breathed from it. Aesc wrapped it in their thickest fur. It slipped in his grip once; he sucked his burnt finger.

They climbed out of the hollow and bowed to Great Mother, giving her thanks.

"Farewell, Aesc. Farewell, Birch. When you leave the island, do not return the way you came. Bear West. If you seek out the Painted people you will have help, if you remain true to your heart, daughter."

"Yes, Great Mother."

They took the holy fire in the dragon's heart and turned towards home.

CHAPTER 6

The ravens flew to meet them. Hugin perched on Aesc's shoulder while Munin settled near to Birch. - Dreki rarely yielded his place to her.

They ate and packed up. Birch bent to pick up a bundle: Ulv's amulet dangled forward from her neck. Munin cried out. She flew at Birch, kaa-ing. Birch waved her arms, trying to drive her off. Why was Munin attacking her? Were they not friends?

"Get away!"

"Munin! What are you doing? Leave Birch alone!" ordered Aesc.

"Kaa Kaa," the she-raven squawked. "Warn! Bad man." She flew to Aesc, then back towards Birch.

"Perch! Now."

Munin obeyed him. Hugin settled beside her.

"Warn," she said.

"Did you hear that?" Aesc asked Birch. "It sounded just like Munin said 'Warn.'"

"I heard no words," replied Birch, dabbing at the scratch on her neck. "I do not understand."

"Neither do I. Are you all right?"

Birch nodded, so they headed for the beach and the boat. Dreki stayed deep down in Birch's hood, even though the birds kept their distance, flying behind.

Aesc spread out his bedding by the fire – on the opposite side to Birch.

"What is wrong, Aesc? You have hardly spoken all day, and now you will not sleep beside me?"

"Would you even miss me?"

"What do you mean?"

"Is there not someone else you would rather lie with?"

"No. What has put this evil into your head?"

"Ulv told me. About you and him."

"What are you saying? How? He is at home."

"No. He hunted with me. Ulv is Ulfhednarr."

"Like the berserks? A shape changer?"

"Yes. Didn't you know?"

"How could I know? I have never seen him hunt. Women chase the mammoths. Men hunt them."

"You gave him my necklace."

"I did not!".

"What else did you give him?"

Fury was a sick, tight ball of fire in Birch's gut.

She slapped him.

Aesc's eyes widened in shock; Birch felt shock, too. She had never felt so fierce before, never struck anyone before.

"He lies! When I see him, I will cut out his false tongue!" She declared.

"Where is the necklace, Birch?"

"I gave it to Great Mother, for the holy flame!"

"But the amulet?"

Birch tore Ulv's amulet from around her neck and flung it into the trees.

"There! Now you will have to walk home!"

Munin fluttered to Birch's shoulder. "Wolf, bad man," she said, glaring at Aesc.

"Birch, forgive me. Forgive me."

The round boat scraped up on the beach. Aesc called out for the Painted boy. He emerged from behind some rocks, a net of edible seaweed in his hand. Aesc bargained with the boy for the loan of his boat. They settled on the price when Aesc included a short spear in the payment. Birch kept a firm grip on her spear: he was not getting that!

The two men struck hands, and the younger one turned towards his home – going West. Birch looked at Aesc. She took two steps after the boy. He looked at her, puzzled. When he continued, Birch and Aesc both followed him. He shrugged, and led on.

His village was made of stacked stones, flat and grey.

"How can they live here?" Birch muttered to Aesc. "How could they go to find food?"

Aesc shook his head and shrugged. "They must manage: they look fed enough."

The Painted people who crowded around their involuntary guide to examine and exclaim over his trade goods did look well. And they fed Birch and Aesc well when evening fell.

A grandmother, wearing feathers in her hair like their own Shaman, offered Birch a bowl of fish and seaweed stew. Her wrinkled eyes stared at her intently. She laid a hand on Birch's belly, smiled, nodded. Birch blinked. What was the old woman telling her? That she was with child? The Dragon had hinted at such. But it was so soon.

Birch's hands prickled: she rubbed them together. Grandmother took her hands and held them. Birch felt the same jolt she felt near her mother's power. The old Shaman's eyes widened. Had she felt it too? Seemingly so: she took one of the feathers from her hair and tied it into Birch's. Birch's stomach fluttered.

When Birch and Aesc lay down together to sleep, she told him what the Shaman had told her. He fell asleep smiling.

Birch dreamed of fish. A huge school, silver, flashing. A standing stone stood overlooking the sea. Its shadow, long in the morning sun, pointed to the sea's bounty. Birch paced out the length of the shadow.

When Birch woke, she hurried to find the grandmother.

The Painted people had looked at the drawings Birch had made for their Shaman. They scurried to find nets and spears and scrambled down the cliffs to their boats. They would have full bellies tonight.

Aesc loaded the food they had been given, and the wrapped Dragon's heart, into the boat which was now theirs. It was long, like their wooden boats, but light like the round boats. If they needed to, they could carry it.

Birch checked that Dreki was with them, and whistled for the ravens. Aesc pushed the boat out into the waves, and turned it towards home.

They paddled down the coast, going ashore at night when they could. Dreki rode with his paws on the bow, like a draconic lookout. Birch wondered how he could: her eyes were aching from the sun glare on the water. When they got to their own country, they went by river, and if the water became too shallow, they carried the boat.

Aesc could see home. He could smell it: cooking smoke blew towards him on the cool breeze. He paddled into the bank, pulled the boat up onto their river beach, and lifted Birch onto land. It was a short walk to their village.

"Wait, Aesc," Birch asked.

She stopped again, and ducked into the stand of birch trees on the bank. As she heaved, Aesc frowned, puzzled. What had made Birch sick? Food went bad sometimes, if the evil spirits meddled with it. Perhaps that was it? But he had eaten the same meal as she last night. It had looked, smelled, and tasted wholesome. There had seemed nothing wrong.

As he waited, he watched Hugin explore the reeds at the river's edge. Idly, Aesc copied the shape his feet made in the river sand, drawing with the point of his spear. Then he drew the trees that shared Birch's name: straight, slim lines. He added shapes to one, to stand for her full breasts and belly that caried their child.

Birch re-joined him.

"Birch, why are you sick?'

"It is the child. No-one knows why."

"Oh," He added: "Nearly home."

Their friends and family crowded round. Words of greeting came from every direction.

"Birch, you are home!"

"Aesc, Birch – welcome back,"

"Yes, I know they are back," said Aunt, "Get the big cooking pit going. We must make a feast."

Birch's mother ran to embrace Birch and her father hugged them both. The Shaman patted Birch on the shoulder and slapped his son on the back. Everywhere there were smiles.

Aesc rubbed his cheeks. "I smile too much; my face aches!"

Birch kissed it better for him.

It was quiet in the Shaman's hut. Birch held the dragon heart stone and Aesc unwrapped it. The Shaman put it in the place of honour in the shrine, next to the newly lit lamp. The holy fire was bright and strong.

Everyone had gathered around the fire pit. (Except Dreki and the ravens. Birch had shut them in her hut, with a private feast of their own, for safety.) Fingers and mouths were greasy with roasted meat, sticky with honey, bright with berry juice. Children ran around squealing and laughing until their parents called them to order.

Aesc wore the shirt that Birch had made for him, the shells glittering in the firelight. Birch's dress was new. She still wore the Shamaness's feather in her hair. Around her neck was the first amber bead of the new necklace that Aesc was making for her. (After he had made her a spear of her own, of course. She would remind him of that.)

Birch and Aesc stood, approached, and bowed to their fathers, the Shaman and the Chieftain.

"Sirs, we have completed the quest that you ordained," said Aesc.

"We have much to tell you," Birch added. Birch caught her mother's gaze, and her hand drifted towards her belly. She smiled.

Aesc stood.

"Hark!" He paused to gather eyes. "I will tell you a story of dragons, of a treasure hoard of magic and skills, of wisdom gained, of courage and love…"

The End

Afterword

How this story came about.
(If you don't want spoilers, read the story first.)

I'd like to say that it all started with fishing for mammoths in the English Channel. That would sound cool, wouldn't it? Actually, the idea for *Dragon's Heart* was initially sparked by a submission call for Specul8 Publishing in Queensland. The publisher, Terry, wanted dragons for his upcoming anthology *Hoards of the Great Fire Wyrms: A Dragon Anthology* (2019). So, dragons I would give him.

But what sort of dragons?

For something that never existed, there are lots of stories, world-wide, about many kinds of dragons. The traditional Mediaeval killed-by-St George kind? Perhaps the flightless Chinese water dragons that bring good luck? Or the original Norse type, like Fafnir? (Killed by Sigurd of the Volsung clan in the late 13th century

Volsunga Saga, an epic poem from Iceland.) Fafnir the dragon was described as a serpentine, flightless dragon, or wyrm. I decided to favour the Norse stories, but make my dragons able to fly.

Okay, so my dragons were set, but what timeline to use for the story? Documentaries are often good for inspiring ideas, as was the one about mammoth-fishing in the English Channel that I had watched just after reading the submission call. This is where my archaeology and traditional literatures degree came in handy. I made a Supposal: What if dragons *were* real once, and were a kind of megafauna, contemporaries of mammoths? This helped me greatly with world building: I could adapt and recreate the real world instead of starting my world from scratch. (Easier, I thought, until I drowned in research.)

So, I asked myself, where and when did megafauna live? More than 12 thousand years ago, at the end of the last Ice Age (Holocene period), when most continents had their own megafauna. Giant sloths and megatheriums had lived in the Americas. Both North America and Australia had giant birds. In Australia there were also once *Thylacaleos* (marsupial 'lions'), and giant wombats, including the *Diprotodon*. And some *humongous* lizards. (Aha!)

Okay, so I had a flying dragon, at the end of the Ice Age. But where to set the story?

Of course, I settled on Northern Europe, as it comprised the future lands of the Viking Norse and the Anglo-Saxons, so 'dragon country'. I chose Doggerland, which once joined continental Europe to future Britain, and is currently under the English Channel, since the sea level is 120 metres higher now. (Yes, the mammoth fishing documentary). Fossils prove the presence of megafauna in the area in the Mesolithic age. Perfect.

Cue My Literature Degree, including the Development of the English Language bit. To transport the reader back in time and create an ancient feel, I attempted to replace any words rooted in the Latin and Greek languages, (e.g., Latin *tunica* – tunic – became Old English *shirt*) and wrote *Dragon's Heart* in sort of-Anglish vocabulary (to the best of my limited ability.). But no prizes to anyone who found the words I missed.

Now, I just needed our main characters. Here, I drew on both archaeology and mythology to create Birch and Aesc. I hypothesised a possible pre-Norse Neolithic culture, and imagined the two main characters as legendary ancestors of, and foreshadowing, the Norse gods.

In the first draft Birch's name was originally Freya, and like dragons and trolls, the goddess Freya is Norse. The tree sacred to Freya is the birch. As I was aiming to pre-date Norse mythology, I decided on the name Birch for my female lead. Odin (Freya's husband in Norse tales and Father of the Norse gods) hung on an ash tree for nine days to learn the secret of the runes and gain added magical knowledge. (Where Odin learnt runes, Aesc invented them.) Odin was the inspiration for Aesc.

There are multiple nods to the Northern cultures in the story, if you're interested. When I was proof reading the text, I found sixteen. How about you?

Acknowledgements

I'd like to thank Gemma Swain who was always there to listen.

This story was originally published in the *Hoards of the Great Fire Wyrms* anthology, published by Specul8 Publishing in 2019. This version is updated from that published in the anthology.

About the Author

SM Kemmett scribbled her first story at seven. She flirted with various careers, but her true passion is wordsmithing. Sharon graduated from Flinders University with a BA in English and Archaeology.

She writes speculative fiction, preferring science fiction, fantasy and steampunk, and dabbles in historical fiction.

She previously volunteered as a tour-guide at the South Australian Museum and is currently volunteering at her neighbourhood library as Local History research editor and blogger.

Sharon lives in much-too-sunny Adelaide.

smkemmettwordtailor.wordpress.com/
amazon.com/author/SMKemmett
Where to buy your eBook copy
books2read.com/b/Dragons-Heart

Follow Sharon at:
www.goodreads.com/smkemmett
www.facebook.com/smkemmettwordtailor/
https://twitter.com/SharonKemmett

OTHER WORKS BY SM KEMMETT

Available in paperback and eBook:
Hemlock Soames and the Waterhorse
Dragon's Heart

www.ingramcontent.com/pod-product-compliance
Lightning Source LLC
Chambersburg PA
CBHW020534120726
47904CB00003B/1080